The Incredible Peepers of
Penelope Budd

✽ ✽ ✽

For my mom, Josie.
—M.K.

*To children of all ages, especially those who always
see beauty and magic in the world.* —A.W.

First Edition
09 08 07 06 05   5 4 3 2 1

Text © 2005 Marie Karns
Illustrations © 2005 Amy Wummer

Published by
Gibbs Smith, Publisher
P.O. Box 667
Layton, Utah 84041

Orders: 1.800.748.5439
www.gibbs-smith.com

Designed by Sheryl Dickert Smith
Printed and bound in Hong Kong

Library of Congress Cataloging-in-Publication Data

Karns, Marie.
The incredible peepers of Penelope Budd / Marie Karns ; illustrations by Amy Wummer. — 1st ed.
p. cm.
Summary: With one brown eye and one blue eye, the unusual Penelope Budd observes things that
others do not see.
ISBN 1-58685-405-4
[1. Eye—Fiction. 2. Imagination—Fiction. 3. Identity—Fiction. 4.
Individuality—Fiction.] I. Wummer, Amy, ill. II. Title.

PZ7.K1444Inc 2005
[E]—dc22
2005007938

The Incredible Peepers of
Penelope Budd

Marie Karns

Illustrated by
Amy Wummer

GIBBS P SMITH

Gibbs Smith, Publisher
Salt Lake City

Penelope Budd was born with eyes the color
of midnight stars and a shock of black hair
that swept across her forehead.

But, at three months of age, one eye turned the color of root beer, while the other eye turned as blue as a lake.

"Hmmm. We'd
better see a doctor,"
Penelope's mother
said, tapping her chin.

The doctor shined a bright light into the incredible peepers of Penelope Budd. She moved a finger side to side, slowly. Penelope's eyes followed.

After more tests, the doctor proclaimed, "Penelope's vision is fine, and her eyes are healthy. Come back if you see more changes. Otherwise, know she's just the way she's supposed to be!"

But after that the incredible peepers of Penelope Budd stayed the same . . .

one the color of hot chocolate, and the
other the color of a forget-me-not.
And people noticed.

What happened to her eye?" Aunt Matilda cried. "It's turned the color of a raisin. I've never seen anything like it!" she said, zooming in for a close-up.

"Look at Junior," said Uncle Frank, tugging his five-year-old's face by the chin. "His two eyes are the same color, like peas. That's the way it should be."

"She's not normal!" they shrieked.

I'll have you know," said Penelope's mother with her hands on her hips, "Penelope Budd is just the way she's supposed to be. She's unique, and she'll see things no other person will see!"

And, oh, the many, amazing, one-of-a-kind things Penelope's incredible peepers saw!

When Grandma cracked eggs into a mixing bowl, out dropped one with two yolks.

"Did you see that?" Penelope
squealed. "An egg with two yolks!"

It whirled through the beaters leaving two streaks
the color of sunshine.

After a rain, Penelope crouched next to a puddle. "Don't play in that filthy mud puddle," Aunt Matilda yelled.

But Penelope saw a giant reflecting pond with a shiny rainbow edge.

"I can see myself in it," she said. "And when I blow on it, my face gets wavy!" Penelope blew on the mud puddle, and Aunt Matilda shook her head.

On a walk to town, Junior said, "Look! Someone dropped a candy and now there are bugs all over it."

But Penelope marveled at the ant parade marching loop-de-loop toward the lollipop. "I think I see the number 8!"

In the summer, Uncle Frank trimmed the
hedges and pulled up dandelions.

"Weeds, weeds, and more weeds, as far as
the eye can see," he said, wiping his forehead
with a hanky.

But Penelope saw bright flowers the color of lemons, and she picked a big bouquet for her mother.

At the beach, all the children built sandcastles.

But Penelope made a giant dragon, using apples for its eyes.

On the drive home from the coast the car windows fogged up, and Penelope discovered she could write her name on the glass just by using her finger.

"My finger is a magic pencil," she said to Junior.

"Penelope," he said, "your finger is just your finger."

"Not to me," she said. And she wrote the word

Later that night Penelope washed her face before bed. She stared at the incredible peepers looking back at her in the mirror.

She winked one way: blue.

She winked the other way: brown.

She blinked:

blue and brown!

*T*ucked in bed, Penelope peered through the window at the night sky. She played connect the dots with the stars.

She found a boot, a bell, and a mushroom.

She saw that the world around her was amazing.

And that's just the way
it's supposed to be!